For Matilda, who could easily tackle a tiger!
– SS

For Guy and Yves, my dearest, magical uncles
– JD

LITTLE TIGER PRESS LTD,
an imprint of the Little Tiger Group
1 Coda Studios, 189 Munster Road, London SW6 6AW
Imported into the EEA by Penguin Random House Ireland,
Morrison Chambers, 32 Nassau Street, Dublin D02 YH68
www.littletiger.co.uk

First published in Spain 2021
This edition published in Great Britain 2022

Text copyright © Steve Smallman 2021
Illustrations copyright © Joëlle Dreidemy 2021
Steve Smallman and Joëlle Dreidemy have asserted their rights to be identified as the
author and illustrator of this work under the Copyright, Designs and Patents Act, 1988
A CIP catalogue record for this book is available from the British Library

All rights reserved · ISBN 978-1-80104-160-7
Printed in China · LTP/1400/3936/0621
10 9 8 7 6 5 4 3 2 1

THE TIGER WHO CAME FOR DINNER

Steve Smallman   Joëlle Dreidemy

LiTTLE TiGER
LONDON

In a cottage, deep in the woods, lived a wolf called Wolf, a lamb called Hotpot and Omelette, their crocodile. They were a rather unusual family, but then the best families often are.

Every day they went for a walk, and every day they played their favourite game.

FETCH!

Morning!

Sometimes Omelette brought back the same stick.

Good boy, Omelette!

Sometimes he brought back a different stick.

Good try, Omelette!

And sometimes he brought back things that weren't sticks at all!

Good grief, Omelette!

One day he brought back . . .

...a little wet tiger.

"Ooh! Hello, Fluffy!" cried Hotpot, giving the soggy tiger a great big hug. "Can we keep her, Woof?"

Wolf shook his head. "Sorry, Hotpot, but this little tiger's family must live further up the river. We have to take her home."

So the next day, that's exactly what they did.
"We're going on a tiger hunt . . ." Wolf sang
as they marched along the river.

Everyone they met thought Fluffy was adorable!
And she was. She was cuddling Hotpot tightly, sniffing
and snuffling behind her ear.

"That tickles!" giggled Hotpot. "Look, Woof, Fluffy loves me!"
    But Omelette wasn't so sure.
Especially when . . .

. . . they met some mice playing tag.
"Can we play?" asked Hotpot.
"Fluffy loves the mice!"

"Grrr!" said Omelette.
Fluffy loved them a bit too much!
She didn't want to let them go.

"Look at the fish jumping, Fluffy!" laughed Wolf.
Fluffy jumped too.
"She loves the fish!" laughed Hotpot.
But no one saw what Omelette saw!

"GRRR!" he growled, flashing his teeth.
Fluffy dropped the fish back into the water.

"That tiger is ADORABLE!" chattered a squirrel.

"Yes," agreed Wolf, "and she loves everybody! Especially Hotpot."
"Fluffy is kissing me!" giggled Hotpot.
Omelette wasn't happy, and no one could understand why.

"Come on, Omelette," smiled Wolf. "Let's play fetch."
And in no time at all, Omelette was happy again.

Later, as the sun began to set, Wolf found a spot to put up the tent.

"Dinner time!" he called. "Who wants carrot soup?"
   "Yummy, yummy," said Hotpot.
'Slurp!' agreed Omelette.

But Fluffy was already chewing on something . . .
Hotpot's tail!

"OUCH!" cried Hotpot.
SNAP, SNAP, SNAP! went Omelette's teeth
towards Fluffy's furry bottom.

"WAAAAGH!" cried the little tiger, bursting into tears.
    "Goodness me!" called Wolf. "What a hullabaloo. I think
we're all a bit tired and hungry. Now, let's say sorry and
have a group hug."

The tiger was still crying a little bit.

But Omelette knew crocodile tears when he saw them.

And while the others drifted off to sleep, Omelette kept one eye open, all night long.

They hadn't gone far the next day
when they came across a cottage.
"What a view!" sighed Wolf.
"Is this your home, Fluffy?"

The little tiger grinned and nodded.
Then she picked up a stick and
threw it into the river!

Omelette leapt in, grabbed it and disappeared over the waterfall's edge!

"What did you do that for, Fluffy?" gasped Wolf. "How could you?"

"Easy peasy!" snarled the little tiger.
"MUM, DAD, I'M HOME!
AND I'VE BROUGHT . . . SUPPER!"

Two hungry looking
tigers came tumbling
out of the cottage.

"Leave her alone!" cried Wolf, holding Hotpot tight.
   "Take no notice of him," sneered the tiger cub.
"He's a big softy."

The tigers grinned and licked their whiskers.
Closer and closer they crept, and were
just about to pounce when . . .

. . . out of the river leapt Omelette! With a very large stick clamped in his very large teeth!.

CRUNCH, CREAK,

SNAP!
went the stick.

"AAAAAAAAAAAAAAARGHHHH!"
cried the tigers.

They grabbed the tiger cub and raced into their shack,
shutting the door with a BANG!

Wolf and Hotpot gave the soggy crocodile a great big hug!

"Home now?" asked Hotpot.

"Home now," agreed Wolf.

So back down the mountain went Wolf and Hotpot with Omelette. He wasn't small or cute - and he would never be fluffy - but he was family, and they loved him.